This is

....'s

book

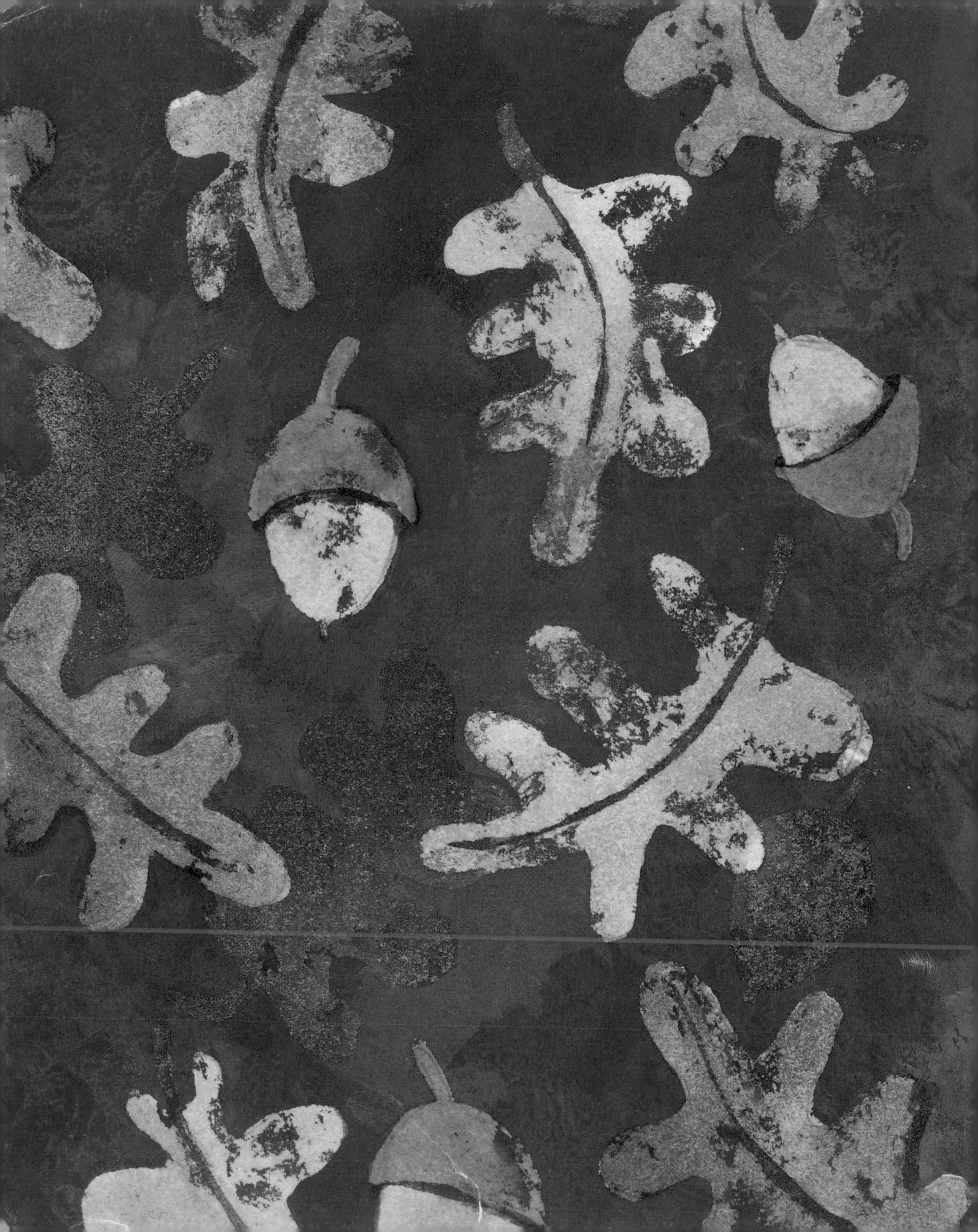

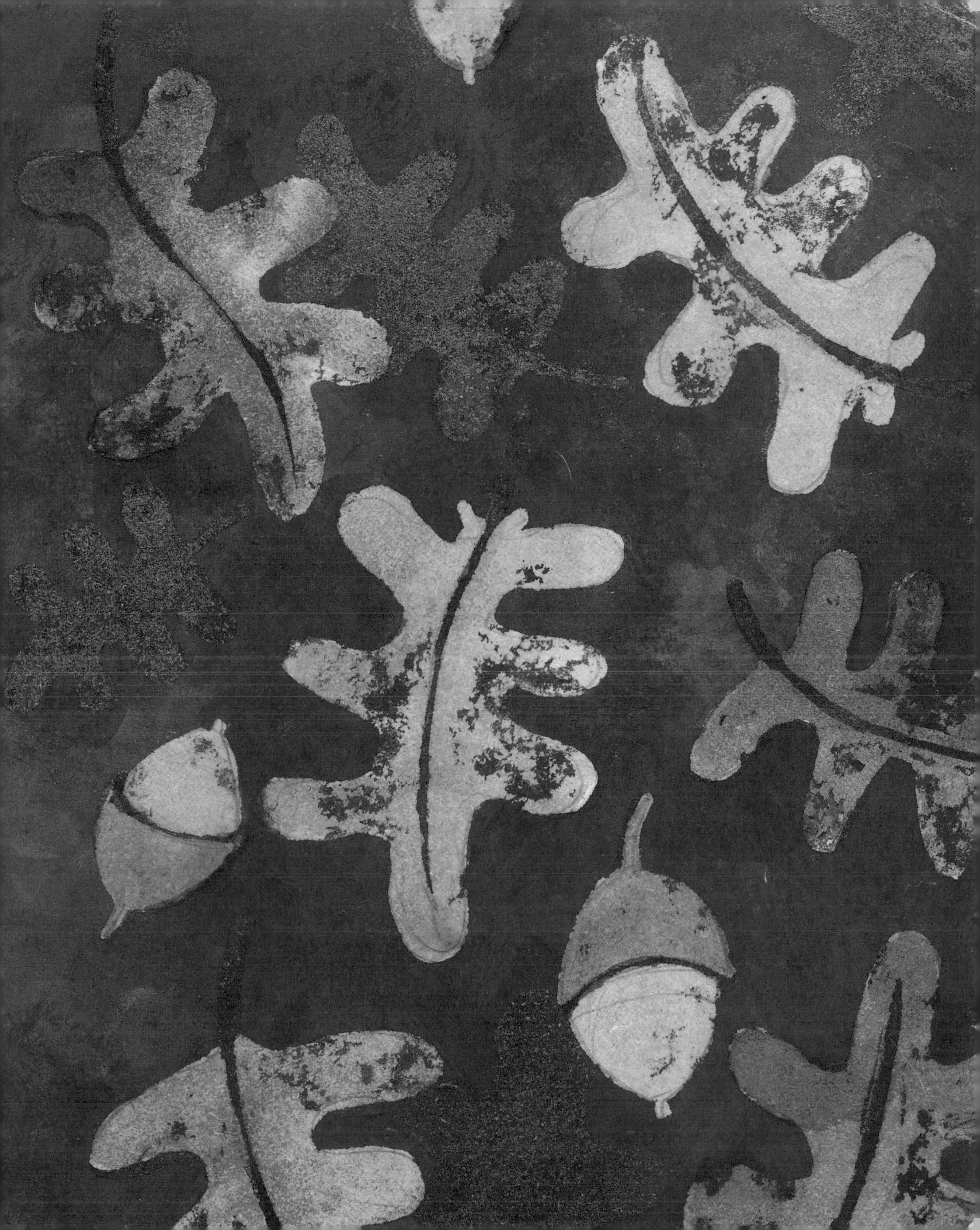

For Mum, Dad and Jane
with love

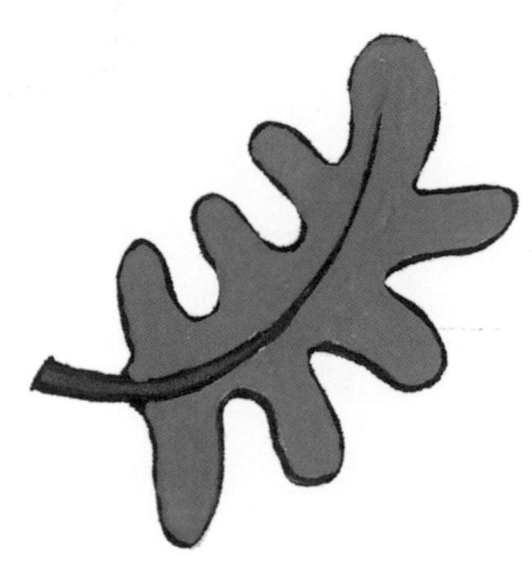

First published in Great Britain in 1994 by ABC

This edition first published in 1994 by softbacks,
an imprint of ABC, All Books for Children,
a division of The All Children's Company Ltd,
33 Museum Street, London WC1A 1LD

Printed and bound in Singapore

British Library Cataloguing in Publication Data
Chicken Little. - New ed
I.Hobson, Sally
823

ISBN 1-85704-057-0

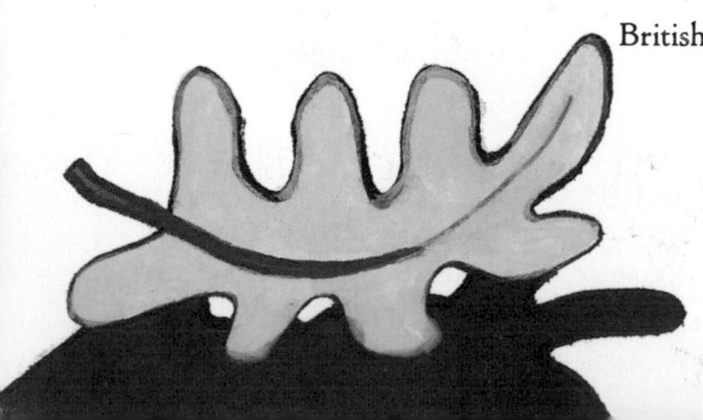

Chicken Little

Sally Hobson

softbacks

One morning, an acorn fell
on Chicken Little's head. PLOP!

Chicken Little looked up.
"The sky is falling," he cheeped.
"I must tell the king."

"Hello," clucked Henny Penny.
"Where are you going in such a hurry?"
"The sky is falling," cheeped Chicken Little, "and I must tell the king."
"Then I will trot with you," clucked Henny Penny, and they set off to find the king.

"Hello," crowed Cocky Locky.
"Where are you going in such a hurry?"
"The sky is falling," cheeped Chicken Little,
"and we must tell the king."

"Then I will strut with you," crowed Cocky Locky, and they set off to find the king.

"Hello," quacked Ducky Lucky. "Where are you going in such a hurry?"

"The sky is falling," cheeped Chicken Little, "and we must tell the king."

"Then I will waddle with you," quacked Ducky Lucky, and they set off to find the king.

"Hello," gaggled Drakey Lakey.
"Where are you going in such a hurry?"

"The sky is falling," cheeped Chicken Little, "and we must tell the king."

"Then I will toddle with you," gaggled Drakey Lakey, and they set off to find the king.

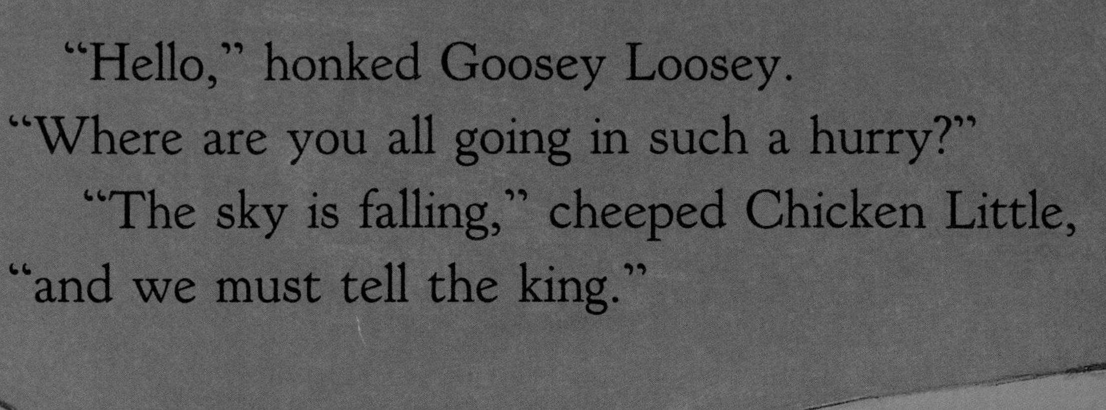

"Hello," honked Goosey Loosey. "Where are you all going in such a hurry?"

"The sky is falling," cheeped Chicken Little, "and we must tell the king."

"Then I will paddle with you," honked Goosey Loosey, and they set off to find the king.

"Hello," gobbled Turkey Lurkey.
"Where are you all going
in such a hurry?"

"The sky is falling," cheeped Chicken Little, "and we must tell the king."

"Then I will march with you," gobbled Turkey Lurkey.

And they set off
to find the king.

"Hello," growled Foxy Loxy. "Where are you going in such a hurry?"

"The sky is falling," cheeped Chicken Little, "and we must tell the king."

"Come with me," growled Foxy Loxy. "I'll take you to the king."

So Chicken Little, Henny Penny,
Cocky Locky, Ducky Lucky,
Drakey Lakey, Goosey Loosey
and Turkey Lurkey followed
Foxy Loxy straight into his
lair — and never came out again.

And Chicken Little never told the king the sky was falling.

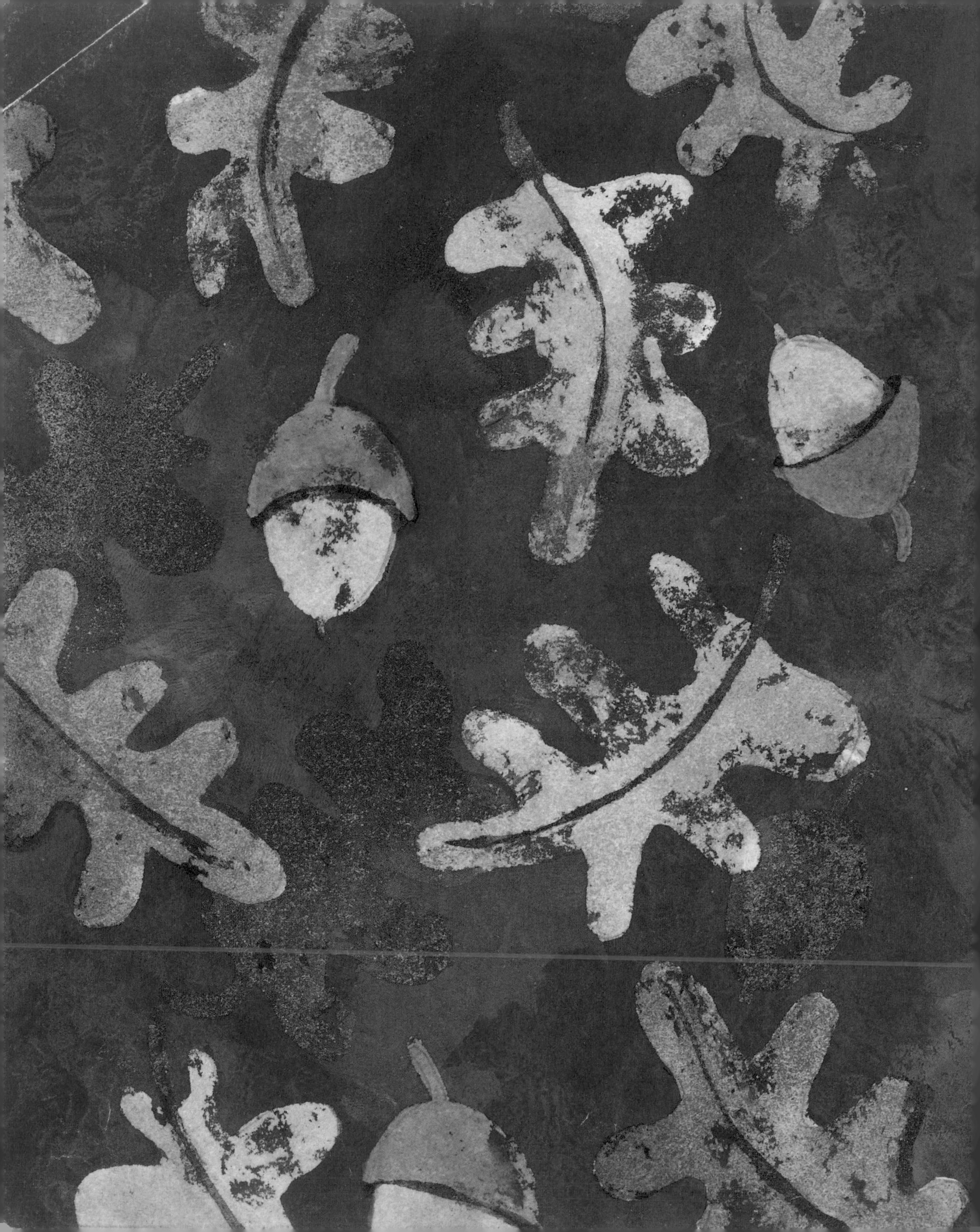